Cookiesaurus Rex

by **Amy Fellner Dominy and Nate Evans**

illustrated by **AG Ford**

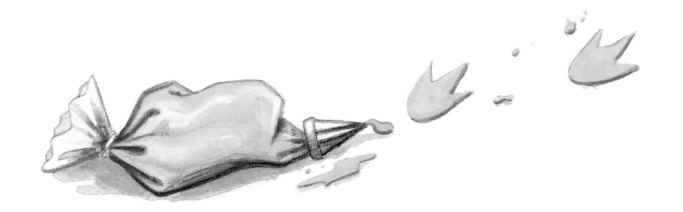

DISNEP · HYPERION

Los Angeles   New York

With special thanks to Mary Wong
for introducing us and always supporting
the writing community in so many ways.
–A.F.D. & N.E.

First Edition, September 2017
10 9 8 7 6 5 4 3 2 1
FAC-029191-17181
Printed in Malaysia
This book is set in Billy/FontSpring
The illustrations were created in watercolor on paper

Library of Congress Cataloging-in-Publication Data

Names: Dominy, Amy Fellner, author. • Evans, Nate, author. • Ford, AG, illustrator.
Title: Cookiesaurus Rex / by Amy Fellner Dominy and Nate Evans ; illustrated by AG Ford.
Description: First edition. • Los Angeles ; New York : Disney-HYPERION, [2017] • Summary: Not satisfied
with his green frosting and little hat, a cookie shaped like a dinosaur demands to be redecorated.
Identifiers: LCCN 2016034300 • ISBN 9781484767443
Subjects: CYAC: Cookies—Fiction. Humorous stories.
Classification: LCC PZ7.D71184 Co 2017 DDC [Fic]—dc23
LC record available at https://lccn.loc.gov/2016034300

Reinforced binding

Visit www.DisneyBooks.com

To Kyle.
We read a lot of dinosaur books
together—this one is for you.
-A.F.D.

For Jenifer—
you're one sweet cookie!
-N.E.

Drumroll, please. . . .

Oh, that's heavy.

Pointy sparkle. Owie ouch ouch.

Whoops, tickle spot. Just a little more . . .

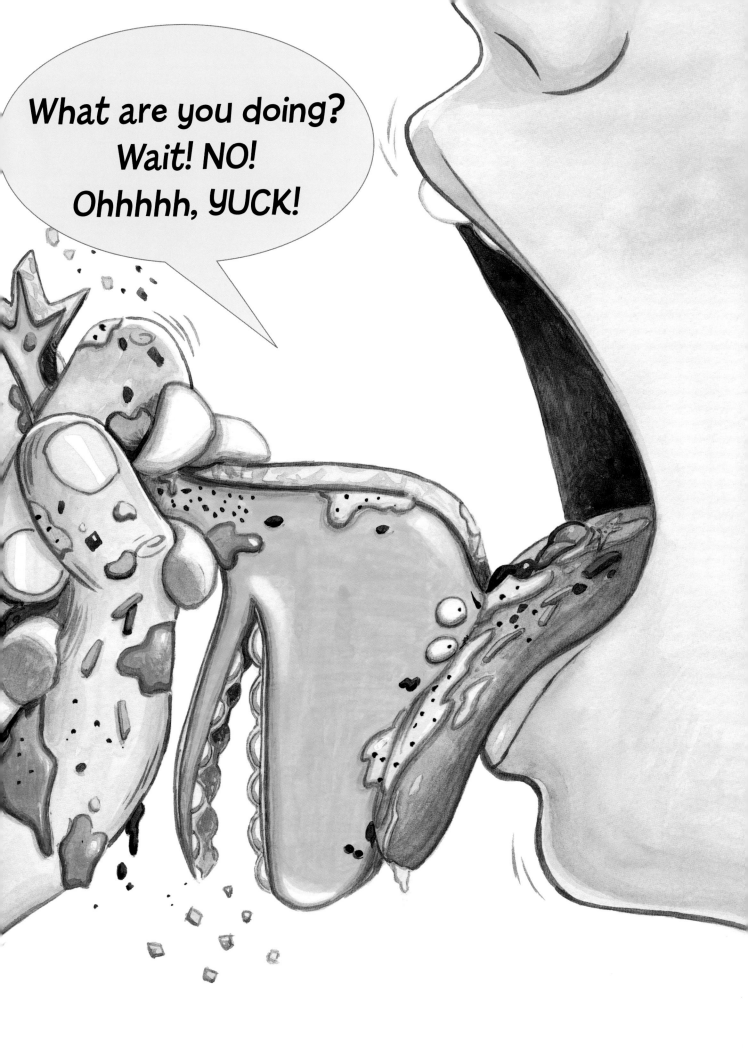